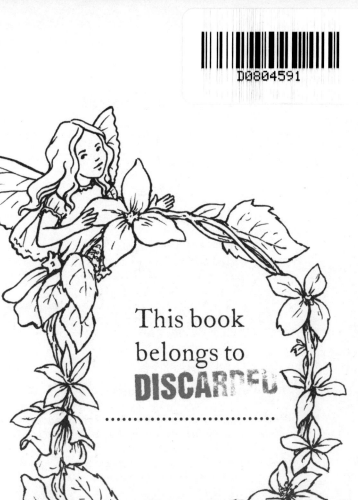

This book
belongs to

....

For Greer, Jack and Seren, with love

FREDERICK WARNE

Published by the Penguin Group
Penguin Books Ltd, 80 Strand, London WC2R 0RL, England
Penguin Young Readers Group, 345 Hudson Street,
New York, New York 10014, U.S.A.
Penguin Books Australia Ltd, 250 Camberwell Road, Camberwell,
Victoria 3124, Australia
Canada, India, New Zealand, South Africa

1 3 5 7 9 10 8 6 4 2

ISBN: 978 07232 5952 7

Printed in Great Britain

Willow's Underwater World

By Kay Woodward

Welcome to the Flower Fairies' Garden!

Where are the fairies?
Where can we find them?
We've seen the fairy-rings
They leave behind them!

Is it a secret
No one is telling?
Why, in your garden
Surely they're dwelling!

No need for journeying,
Seeking afar:
Where there are flowers,
There fairies are!

Contents

Chapter One

Trouble in Flower Fairyland   I

Chapter Two

Flood!   II

Chapter Three

The Investigation Begins   2I

Chapter Four

A Daring Rescue   37

Chapter Five

The Dambusters   5I

Chapter Six

The Mystery is Solved   63

Chapter One
Trouble in Flower Fairyland

"By the peaceful stream or the shady pool
I dip my leaves in the water cool.
Over the water I lean all day,
Where the sticklebacks and the minnows play.
I dance, I dance, when the breezes blow,
And dip my toes in the stream below."

Singing merrily to herself, Willow shimmied down the long, bendy branch to the stream beneath her tree. The graceful Flower Fairy looked for her stepping stone. This was where she loved to perch, balancing on one foot while she dipped the other into the greeny-blue water.

The stepping stone wasn't there.

"How odd . . ." mused Willow. "I saw it yesterday." With nowhere to rest her feet, she decided to fly back. So, she wiggled her long, elegant gossamer wings—which were palest green, like the leaves of her tree—and fluttered to the safety of a higher branch. There, she sat to ponder the mystery of the disappearing stone. Had it been swept away?

She doubted it—the stone was big and wedged in the sludgy riverbed. Willow knew this because she'd swum to the very bottom of the stream last summer. She'd been hunting for hazelnuts that a picnicking Flower Fairy had accidentally dropped into the water, but she'd taken the opportunity to have a good look around. Willow was an excellent swimmer.

From the top of her tree she had a bird's-eye view of the stream and the Flower Fairies who visited its banks. There was Iris, a sweet, shy fairy whose sunny yellow flowers grew in the shallows. Many other fairies visited simply to dip their toes in the deliciously cool water. Lavender came here often too. She loved nothing better than to scrub her clothes with magical soap, before rinsing them in the rushing water.

And that was when Willow noticed. Apart from a ripple or two, the stream hardly seemed to be flowing at all. If anything, the water level was *rising*. As far as she knew, this only happened after a sudden shower—and it had been dry and sunny for a week. She peered downwards and, sure enough, her stepping stone was now totally submerged by a depth of at least two acorns. How could the water have got so deep so quickly?

Blip-blop!

A shimmering golden
fish leapt above the surface.
"Why, hello, Mr Stickleback!"
Willow called. "Do *you* know what's going
on?"

But the fish didn't answer her. He dived
beneath the water with a *splash* and vanished.

Willow frowned. Was the fish shy or
scared or did he just want to be alone? She
couldn't tell. Something was afoot—but
what? She pushed her long honey-blonde
hair from her eyes and gazed upstream,
to where the glittering ribbon of water
stretched towards the edge of the Flower
Fairies' Garden and beyond. The Flower
Fairy was used to keeping an eye on the
stream. As the official lookout, it was
her job to warn the others of new arrivals

to the garden. But there were no clues upstream today. And her view downstream was blocked by the tumbling leaves of the weeping willow tree. No matter—she would embark upon an extensive search. Perhaps some of the other fairies would help out.

"Yoohoo!" she called, cupping her hands around her mouth to make sure the sound travelled as far as the water's edge. "Iris! Are you busy?"

The timid Flower Fairy looked up and blushed. "Er . . . not really," she said guiltily. "I was just, um . . . Well, the water's surface is so smooth today that it's almost as good as a mirror."

Willow grinned, amused by the fact that her pretty friend was so embarrassed at being caught checking out her reflection.

By now, Iris's cheeks were rosier than ripe tomatoes. "All done," she said quickly, before taking one last peek at the water. "*Arggghhhhh!*" she screamed as she sprang to her feet and—with a sprinkle of fairy dust to make her fly faster—zoomed up and away from her flower-laden plant.

"What's wrong?" cried Willow, quickly sliding down the branches before leaping the

gap between the leaf tips and the bank. She hurried across to where Iris cowered beneath the spiky blackthorn bush—bare of petals now that summer was on its way—and flung a comforting arm around her dear friend's shoulders. "What is it?" she asked. "Tell me, please."

"B-b-big eyes!" stammered Iris, her own eyes wide with horror.

"*What* has big eyes?" asked Willow.

'Sh-sh-sharp teeth!" By now, Iris was trembling wildly.

"*Who?*" Willow said desperately. She hated to see her friend so upset.

"F-f-fish!" cried Iris at last.

"Oh, you mean Mr. Stickleback!" Willow clapped her hands together with relief. "The fish whose beautiful golden scales glint in the sunlight? Don't worry about him—he means no harm."

Iris shook
her head slowly.
"I know Mr.
Stickleback," she
whispered. "Th-this
was a monster of a fish.
It had a pointy head and
grey-green scales and eyes as
b-b-big as Mallow's fairy cheeses. It swam
right up to me and opened its jaws so wide
that I thought it would swallow me up!" She
burst into tears, burying her face in the leafy
handkerchief that Willow quickly pushed
into her hands.

"Please don't worry," said Willow. All the
same, she was rather puzzled. She'd never
seen such a creature in Flower Fairyland.
"Thousands of fish swim downstream every
year," she added. "By the time you dry your
eyes, the scary fish will be long gone."

Chapter Two
Flood!

Willow led the way, marching purposefully towards the stream to show that there was nothing to be scared of. But despite her outwardly brave appearance, her stomach was churning. Something just didn't feel right. Iris followed on behind, biting her fingernails.

Splash! Willow looked down in surprise to see that she was ankle-deep in water. *Splosh!* Iris joined her. Totally bemused, the two Flower Fairies stared at each other.

"I don't remember there being a puddle here..." said Iris.

"Me neither," said Willow.

"That's no puddle!" called Cornflower as he skipped past—a blur of brightest blue. In his hand was a small boat made from a folded celandine leaf, with a petal for a sail. "The stream has broken its banks. This is a *flood!*"

It was true. Even as they watched, water was washing over the edges of the stream. Fingers of water were stretching further and further over dry land—soon they would cover the grass and the small fairy pathways that criss-crossed over it.

"Wonderful, isn't it?" continued Cornflower. He set his home-made boat on the water and blew it along, paddling after it as it gathered speed. "It's like having our very own Flower Fairy boating lake!"

"Er ... Cornflower!" cried Willow. She hated to sound like the grown-up humans she'd heard in the garden, but she had to warn

him. Cornflower was well known for his adventurous nature and she didn't want him to come to harm. "Be careful, won't you? It's dangerous to play near rivers and streams and you're getting so close to the edge—"

Too late.

Cornflower stepped from the shallow edge straight into the depths of the stream, vanishing beneath the water with

a loud *bloop*. He reappeared almost as quickly, shooting out of the water as if he'd bounced on an underwater trampoline. The sodden Flower Fairy scrambled and splashed away

from the deeper
water on his hands
and knees. He wore
an expression of pure
terror.

"What—was—that?"
he gasped, struggling upright.
He looked a terrible state. The star-
shaped flowers that clustered in his hair
and decorated his outfit hung limply, while
his pretty blue butterfly wings drooped,
droplets of water dripping from the tips.

"What was *what*?" asked Willow
carefully. She seemed to be having the same
conversation over and over today. And, deep
down, she had a horrible feeling that she
already knew what her fairy friend had seen.

"The monster!" Cornflower wailed. "It
had the most wickedly sharp teeth and the
biggest eyes that I've ever seen. I'm never

going in the water again! I *hate* the boating lake!" And he burst into tears.

"There, there . . ." said Willow, who couldn't stand to see anyone upset. If fairies wept for too long, she was likely to join in. "Don't worry, we'll get to the bottom of this." She turned to Iris. "Do you have any spare fairy dust on you? We need to work some magic on this poor Flower Fairy."

"But of course," said Iris at once. She reached into the folds of her sunshine-yellow petal dress, taking a small silken bag from a hidden pocket. She pulled the bag's drawstring to reveal the glittering fairy dust inside. "How much do you need?"

"Just a pinch," Willow replied. She was delighted to see that the anxious look had faded from Iris's face. She had more than enough fairy dust herself, but knew that her friend needed to stop worrying about the fishy monster that still lurked in the depths of the stream. That problem could wait. First, they needed to cheer up the shivering Cornflower. Quickly, she took a pinch of her own fairy dust—made from the ground-up leaves of the weeping willow tree—and held it above Cornflower's head. She gestured to Iris to do the same. "Ready?" she asked.

"Ready," replied Iris, her pale pink wings

quivering with excitement.

And together they chanted, *"Fairy dust, fairy dust, make him toasty and dry!"* They threw the precious fairy dust high into the air and watched spellbound as the tiny particles tumbled downwards, glittering and shining as they landed on every bit of Cornflower's dripping hair, drooping wings, sodden clothes and damp skin.

"Wow . . ." breathed Cornflower. The cold wet feeling had gone—and all the water too. The magic had even dried his tears. He patted his petal tunic and shorts to make totally sure and grinned widely. "What a smashing thing to do!" he said. "I would never have thought of using fairy dust to dry myself. I'd still have been soaking wet at bedtime!"

Willow smiled. She was thrilled to see that Cornflower had stopped shivering too.

"Glad to be of service!" she said happily.

But Cornflower put his hands on his hips and looked solemn. "Now, I insist on returning the favor," he announced. "I will help you to solve the mystery of the flood and to catch the wicked creature that is tormenting Flower Fairyland. That's what I'll do." He licked his lips thirstily. "Now, who would like a beechnut of elderflower juice while we make a plan?"

Chapter Three
The Investigation Begins

Word spread quickly through Flower Fairyland. It wasn't every day that there was something so momentous as a flood and soon quite a crowd had gathered at the water's edge.

"What's the problem?" said Honeysuckle. "I live way up high—the water's never going to reach me." And he played a quick tune on the flowery trumpet that hung from his belt.

But some of the younger fairies were quite worried.

"What if the whole garden is flooded?" said an anxious Strawberry. "My plant grows so close to the ground that it will be washed away—and me with it!"

"Me too," added Daisy, whose flowers lived among the short grass. She burst into tears.

"Then you shall both come and stay at my place," announced Honeysuckle, as if it were the most obvious thing in the world. "There's plenty of room. Everyone's welcome!"

There were murmurs of gratitude from the crowd of fairies, who were now ankle deep in water. The flood was rising fast. It was time to move to higher ground.

Meanwhile, an intrepid trio of Flower Fairies sploshed downstream, making their way slowly through the flood. Willow, Iris

and Cornflower held sturdy mulberry twigs,
which they prodded in front of them as they
paddled to follow the edge of the stream
—and to avoid tumbling in.

It was Iris who first heard the sound.
"What was that?" she hissed, splashing to a
halt. "I think it was ..."

"*Tee hee!*"

"... children," Cornflower finished. "That's
all we need. A flood, a monster and now

human children!" He tutted and shook his head crossly. "Can it get any worse?"

"Shhhh," said Willow. She was a fairy who believed in magic, but not coincidences. There were too many strange things happening in the Flower Fairies' garden today—she didn't think for a second that they were unconnected. "Let's find out what's going on," she whispered, pointing in the direction of the new sound.

The laughter grew louder. It became clear that there were two voices, belonging to a girl and a boy. They giggled and shouted, splashed and crashed. What *were* they up to?

Slowly, surely, and with as little splish-splashing as possible, the three fairies went onwards. They all knew about humans. Children especially were said to be very nosy and loved to hunt for fairies at the end of the garden. Willow, Iris and Cornflower had

learnt at a very young age about the Flower
Fairy Law, which said that fairies should
stay out of sight of humans at all times. But
it didn't mean that they couldn't watch them
from the safety of a flower or a leafy bush . . .

"Sarah, throw me the biggest one you can
find!" called the boy. His blond hair was
ruffled and his face pink with excitement.

"Ooof!" puffed the girl. "Will this do?"

"Perfect."

Careful not to rustle any leaves, the three Flower Fairies crept right through the fuchsia bush—waving to Fuchsia, who crouched among the new buds—and peeped out the other side.

"So *that's* what's going on," breathed Willow. She watched in astonishment as the two children piled more and more stones into the water, adding to the enormous pile that stretched right across the stream to form a dam. Apart from a few tiny trickles of water, the stream was completely blocked!

"No wonder the stream's flooding," whispered Cornflower. "If the water can't flow downstream, it's got nowhere to go but over the banks. And if the water can't escape, neither can the monster fish!"

"Soon the whole Flower Fairies' Garden will be underwater!" said Iris. "What about the fairies who can't swim? Will the monster gobble them up?" For the second time that day, she burst into tears.

Willow gulped. Suddenly,

everything seemed very scary indeed. Flower Fairies were no bigger than a human hand— how could they hope to move stones and rocks that were larger than themselves?

"Matt!" called Sarah, brushing strands of browny-red hair from her eyes. "What will happen to all the water behind the dam?"

"Oh, it'll probably just trickle away," said Matt. He plugged a hole in the dam with a small piece of rock. "But to make sure, we'll be sure to dismantle the rocks before teatime—Uncle Andrew might be a bit cross if we flood his lawn."

Willow smiled at the other fairies. "What a relief!" she said. The elegant Flower Fairy smoothed her hands on her leafy dress—her palms had grown quite damp with worry. She peered up through the dark green foliage of the fuchsia. "It's well past midday," she guessed, using the position of the sun as a

guide. "Sarah and Matt will soon take the
dam apart, the stream will flow again, the
flood will vanish and the fish will swim away.
It will all be sorted by bedtime." Willow felt
so sure everything would be fine that she
added, "I promise."

At this, both Iris and Cornflower relaxed.
Even Fuchsia ventured down from her hiding
place to watch the children as they played in
the stream. Together, the four Flower Fairies
watched as Sarah and Matt completed their

project, bunging holes in the dam with moss
and twigs. The fairies had to admit that they
were doing a pretty good job of blocking the
stream. It was just a shame that they didn't
realize what havoc they were causing at the
other end of the garden.

"Sarah! Matthew!"

The children looked up as a deep voice
called in the distance.

"It's Uncle Andrew. Come on, we'd better
be quick!" said Matt.

"But what about the dam?" asked Sarah.

"Easy-peasy," said Matt. "Look, all we have to do is knock these bigger stones off and the whole thing will come crashing down." He pointed at the rocks that ran along the top of the dam and aimed a kick at a small boulder. It didn't budge. He tried again. Nothing.

"Sarah? Matthew, where are you? Your snack's ready!"

"Quick!" said Sarah. She rushed over to help, and together, the two children managed to push the boulder from the dam. It fell with a huge splash, leaving a gap through which the stream began to trickle.

Safely hidden from sight among the leaves of the fuchsia, the Flower Fairies cheered silently, then hugged each other with delight. But their celebrations were cut short.

"Children!"

"Come on," said Matt. "We'd better go."

"But we can't leave it like this," said Sarah anxiously.

"We'll come back later," promised the boy. "Hurry up—I'm starving!"

Reluctantly, with one last look over her shoulder at the nearly perfect dam, Sarah followed him past the fuchsia bush and out of sight. There was a shocked silence as the Flower Fairies looked at the barely trickling dam.

Willow gulped. She knew that the gap wasn't big enough to allow all the trapped water to escape. And although the flood may not get any deeper, the water would probably not go down in a hurry. Something drastic needed to be done to return the Flower Fairies' Garden to normal. But what?

"Look!" said Iris. She pointed upstream. There, floating merrily on the top of the water was a procession of small, strange greeny-brown objects. They were shaped like the ice-cream cones that children ate, only much, much smaller. And unlike real ice-cream cones, they sparkled and shone with twinkly fairy dust. "Ooh!" Iris announced. "They look like some sort of magic beads! I wonder where they've come from?"

The tiny cones bobbed towards the dam, but didn't tumble though the gap. Instead,

they became trapped behind a large stone.

Iris burst into tears for a third time. (She was a very emotional Flower Fairy. By now, her willow leaf was quite sodden with tears.) "We must save the magic beads from the monster!" she cried.

Chapter Four
A Daring Rescue

Because nothing like this had ever happened in the Flower Fairies' Garden before, Kingcup and Queen of the Meadow decided to call an emergency meeting. Petal posters were pinned on to trees, proclaiming: *Flower Fairyland Needs You!* And fairies travelled from far and wide to be there—they'd all heard about the flood and wanted to do all they could to help. At precisely four puffs of

Dandelion's seed clock, everyone gathered
on a hillock near Lavender's fragrant plant.
It was one of the few areas of high ground
left at that end of the garden.

"Greetings!" A deep, booming voice
interrupted the excited chatter and the
Flower Fairies turned at once to see Kingcup
perched on the uppermost branches of the
weeping willow. He wore his best outfit of
shimmering gold, with a crown of yellow
flower stamens balanced on his golden hair.

Beside the king was Queen of the Meadow, clad in a beautiful ivory gown. A cloud of flaxen hair framed her pretty face. She waved regally at the crowd. "Thank you so much for coming," she said. "But before we begin, great thanks must go to Willow, who has kindly offered to host this meeting at her lovely home."

Everyone clapped politely and Willow blushed and smiled shyly.

"As I see it," continued Kingcup, "the problems are threefold. Firstly, we have a dam that is causing a flood situation. Secondly, a mighty fish is trapped in the floodwaters and is thus prevented from travelling on its way downstream. Thirdly, mysterious "magic beads" are also caught behind the dam. He turned and nodded to the queen.

"What we must do is this," Queen of the Meadow said. "We must dismantle the dam, so the stream may flow freely once more and free the mighty fish. But first, we must rescue the magic beads and restore them to their rightful owner." She looked around the gathered Flower Fairies. "Do you agree?"

There were resounding cheers of approval.

"Then it's settled," said Kingcup. "Willow

has volunteered to lead a rescue mission to recover the magic beads." He paused for the round of applause. "Who would like to lend a hand?"

Immediately, a sea of waving hands shot into the air. The king pondered his decision for a moment before pointing to Red Campion, a cheerful fairy who lived by the woodland's edge. "You've come a long way," said Kingcup. "Would you like to help?"

Red Campion nodded so hard that his

scarlet hood wobbled violently and looked in danger of falling off. Then he careered madly, leaping and flapping all the way over to Willow, his scarlet-green wings glowing in the late-afternoon sunlight.

Queen of the Meadow nodded to Iris and smiled. "Willow has specially requested that you should be involved," she said softly. "Would you like to do that?"

"Oh yes!" said Iris at once. 'I'd love to." She glanced over at her yellow blossoms, which were just peeping above the water—and sighed. "It'll help me to stop worrying about my poor plant too." With a flutter of her pearly pink wings, she rose into the air and zipped over to Willow and Red Campion, her toes skimming the cool water.

Kingcup addressed the crowd once more. "While the rescue team proceeds with their mission," he said, "the queen and I welcome suggestions for dealing with the dam. Any ideas?"

With the sounds of the eager crowd of Flower Fairies fading behind them, Willow,

Red Campion and Iris made their way to a spot of dry land. Willow was prepared for adventure and carried with her a large bundle carefully wrapped in old leaves. She couldn't wait to share her plan with the others.

"So what do you have there?" asked Red Campion, jiggling on the spot enthusiastically. "A super-long lasso? A year's supply of fairy dust? It *is* something we can use to rescue the magic beads, isn't it?"

Willow nodded. "It's a boat," she announced, with a huge, satisfied grin.

The other two looked deeply uncertain. "A boat?" they chorused.

"But it's not big enough,' said Iris. 'It's the wrong shape."

"Aha!" Willow unwrapped the bundle and revealed a collection of long, bendy twigs and some large, glossy leaves— all had come from her own tree.

"That's not a boat," said Red Campion, looking hugely disappointed. "It's a bonfire." When he realized how rude he'd been, his cheeks turned as red as his outfit. "Sorry . . ." he mumbled.

Willow pretended to look shocked and hurt, but she couldn't keep a straight face and her mouth curled into a grin. "Just you wait and see," she said, swiftly laying out the twigs in a rough circle. "Iris, can you help me to tie these willow twigs together with long grasses? We're going to make a boat frame."

Iris nodded vigorously. "Of course," she said. And for the first time since the stream flooded, she began to look happy again.

"Red Campion," said Willow, turning to him. 'We're going to use these leaves to cover the frame and make the boat watertight."

"Roger, boss," said the eager Flower Fairy, his pointy ears wiggling eagerly. His embarrassment was quite forgotten.

They all set to work, bending and

45

twisting the twigs before knotting them tightly in position. The leaves were carefully overlapped to make sure there were no gaps for water to trickle inside. And, in as little time as it takes to dance a fairy jig, it was finished. The boat was unlike any that Iris and Red Campion had ever seen.

"It's shaped like a mixing bowl!" exclaimed Red Campion.

Willow giggled. 'I've never thought of it

like that," she said. "Usually, I make paddles to move the boat through the water, but we have no time to carve them, so instead we'll use our hands. Hop in," she said. "There's room for three!"

Iris and Red Campion didn't need telling twice. Willow pushed them away from dry land before leaping into the boat herself. "Altogether now . . . row!" she said.

Luckily for the Flower Fairies, there was a slight current, which carried them gently downstream. Here, the magic beads waited patiently for them, caught above the dam between two rocks. Ever so carefully, Willow leaned over the edge of the boat, leaning closer and closer, so close she could almost touch the magic beads when—

Bump!

The round boat shook alarmingly and the three fairies looked at each other in horror.

They held on tightly as water slopped over
the side, each wondering desperately what
had just happened. Had they collided with
something? Had they run aground?

Bump! Bump!

This time, Willow was looking over the
edge of the boat when it happened, so she
saw the monster pike swim through the clear
water and charge at them. And when he hit,
she lost her grip and shot into the air. There
was no time to flap her wings, no time to do
anything other than grab a handful of fairy
dust and throw it on to the surface of the
stream, before she plunged in after it. She
sank like a stone.

Chapter Five

The Dambusters

Meanwhile, the rest of the Flower Fairies had come up with some inspired ideas for clearing the dam, which could not be shifted by fairy hands alone.

Sycamore, who loved to swing and somersault among the uppermost leaves of his plant, had the idea of dropping objects from a very great height on to the stones. Lavender had an even better idea—why not ask the birds to help? When the others agreed, she and Sycamore sped away to speak with the swallows.

Rose offered to pull out the smaller stones and pieces of moss that plugged the tiniest holes.

"Good thinking," said Queen of the Meadow, with an approving nod. "Every little helps!"

Pear Blossom had the best suggestion of all. "What we need to do is dislodge the stones at the very top of the dam," he said sensibly. "If we move those, at least the stream will be able to flow again." He held aloft a sturdy stick. "We can use the twigs from my tree to lever the stones up and over the dam. It'll be much easier than pushing them."

"Great idea!" cried Kingcup. "Let's get started!"

As an experienced swimmer, Willow could easily have swum back to the surface, but in the split-second before hitting the water, she'd known that now was the perfect opportunity to make a new friend. The fairy dust that she sprinkled on to the water formed a magical entry point to the stream and as she plunged through the fairy dust, Willow felt her lungs fill with air.

Hurray! she cheered silently as she sat at the very bottom of the stream, her long honey-blonde hair streaming outwards. The fairy dust had worked its magic, allowing her to hold her breath for three enchanting minutes underwater. She was very lucky.

Not every Flower Fairy could use this magic. It was only because she lived by the stream that she had such a strong connection with the water. *I don't have much time*, she thought. *Where is that pike?*

Right here, little fairy, said an echoey voice.

Bravely, Willow turned round to see

the mighty fish. Up close, his scales were dazzling and his eyes weren't as big as fairy cheeses—they were much, much bigger. As for his teeth . . . Well, Willow was doing her best not to look at *those*.

You can hear me? asked the pike curiously.

Er . . . yes. Willow realized that she and the fish were talking to each other with their thoughts. Yet more fairy magic! *Pleased to meet you, Mr. Pike.*

Likewise, I'm sure. The pike gave a friendly nod. *I'm terribly sorry that I headbutted your boat. I've been trying to get past the dam and I mistook you for a rock.*

Willow smiled back, making sure to keep her mouth firmly closed so no water trickled inside. She'd been sure the fish meant no harm and was delighted to be proved right. *I just wanted to tell you that we're doing our best to get rid of the dam*, she thought. *You'll soon be free to continue on your journey.*

The pike grinned fishily. *Thank you, kind Flower Fairy.*

With a start, Willow realized that her magic was running out. *Goodbye!* she thought. *The fresh air is calling me.*

Goodbye! replied the pike. And, with gentle nudges of his pointy nose, he pushed the fairy towards the surface.

Willow popped above the water like a cork and grinned at the surprised and relieved looks Iris and Red Campion wore. "You're safe!" they cried. "Quick! Climb in before the monster gets you!"

"He's not a monster," said Willow, clambering into the boat. "He's a friend." It was only after telling the tale of her underwater adventure that she noticed the small, cone-shaped objects rolling around their feet. "You rescued the magic beads!"

she cried.

The fairies nodded proudly, but then Iris
blushed. "Actually, they washed into the boat
when the pike banged into us," she admitted.

"Yoohoo!"

The three Flower Fairies swivelled round
to see who had called. It was Pear Blossom,
riding towards them on the
back of a friendly duck.
He brandished a twig
in the air, looking
like a fairy-tale
prince charging into
battle. "All clear!" he

shouted.

"You might want to paddle to the side," continued Pear Blossom. "The rescue operation is about to kick off. I'm going to lever this stone right off the dam!" Carefully, he stuck his twig into the gap below a large grey stone. He leaned on the twig. Nothing happened.

"Can we help?" asked Willow politely. They'd moved only a short distance away and she'd realized that Pear Blossom was having difficulties.

Pear Blossom rolled up his sleeves and leaned harder. Nothing. Eventually, he looked up and pushed his white-blond fringe from his eyes. "It's very difficult," he said.

Can you give me a hand?" At once, Willow leapt into the air and hovered above Pear Blossom, before jumping on to the end of the stick. It did the trick. Slowly, the stone toppled and then crashed into the stream below. The stream surged through the gap.

"Let's do another!" cried Pear Blossom.

After three stones, a very strange thing began to happen. The force of the water rushing over the dam was enough to dislodge more and more stones.

"Goodbye, Mr. Pike!" called Willow as the fish swam past. "Safe journey!" As Willow had promised, everything was back to normal by bedtime. And when the children crept into the garden at twilight to deal with the dam, they couldn't believe their eyes.

"It's gone," whispered Sarah. "Do you think it was the fairies?"

"No, of course not," replied Matt. "That is, I don't think so . . ."

Chapter Six
The Mystery is Solved

The Flower Fairies had restored their garden to normal, but still no one knew who owned the magic beads. It was a total mystery.

Willow didn't want the beads to get lost, so she decided to put them in a safe place— and the safest place she knew was under the ground near the stream. "No one will disturb them here," she said as she patted a thin layer of soil on top.

Just a few weeks later— and to everyone's surprise —the magic beads sprouted, pushing new shoots up through the soil.

"Well, I never!" said Willow to herself. "They were seeds all along . . ."

When summer was at its hottest, the flowers suddenly bloomed. The blossoms were truly magnificent—yellow and dark red bursts of flame. But they were still a mystery. Nobody knew what the flowers were. Nobody knew how to find their owner. Some of the younger fairies made posters that read: *Have you seen this Flower Fairy?* and *Who lives in a flower like this?* and simply *Help!*

One fine day, Willow was sitting in her tree, decorating a brand-new dress with red ribbon. She was concentrating so hard that she didn't see the newcomer until he was right under her tree.

"At last!" gasped the Flower Fairy, who wore the most fantastically colorful outfit Willow had ever seen. His hair was ginger, his tunic was yellow and flame red, his wings

were deep brown and his shorts were silver. On his feet were matching silver boots with long, pointy toes. He was magnificent. He looked just like—

"My flowers! I've found you at last!" the fairy cried.

Eagerly, Willow slid down a long slender branch to the ground and introduced herself.

"Pleased to meet you, Willow," said the mystery fairy. "I'm Gaillardia. And thank you so much for tending my flowers. I'm more pleased than words can say."

Willow smiled shyly. But there was something she had to find out. "I hope you don't think me rude, but—"

"You're wondering why I became separated from my

flowers, aren't you?" said Gaillardia. "It's a fair question and one that I'd be delighted to answer."

The story didn't take long to tell. Gaillardia had wanted to move to the Flower Fairies' Garden for a very long time—he'd heard it was a wonderful place to live—and that spring, he had packed up his seeds ready to go. But on the long journey, he'd taken a nap beside the stream. When he awoke the seeds were gone. For a while, he thought the birds had eaten them, but then he realized that they must have fallen into the stream and floated away. Ever since, he'd been following the stream in search of his seeds.

"I never expected to find them so well cared for," he said, "and in full bloom too. Thank you so much, Willow."

At this, Willow burst into tears.

Gaillardia patted her shoulder. "There, there,' he said, looking concerned. "What did I say?"

"Oh, it's nothing you said," Willow sobbed. "This is what happens when I'm happy. You see, everyone thinks that the weeping willow gets its name because the leaves weep with sadness. But it's possible to weep with happiness too. And that's why I'm weeping now—because I'm so incredibly happy that everything's turned out so well." She hiccupped loudly and gave a watery smile. "Welcome to the Flower Fairies' Garden!" she said.

Gaillardia fitted right in. He loved the hustle and bustle of the garden and he especially liked living next door to Willow—they

soon became the best of friends. There was
nothing he liked better than listening to the
elegant fairy tell the story of how his seeds
were rescued and the monster pike was
set free. In fact, it was Gaillardia's idea to
celebrate the anniversary of the events with a
willow-boat race across the stream.

It was a marvellous day. Willow judged

the boat race and congratulated a very proud
Red Campion on his win. Then the garden's
newest resident stood up to make a speech.

Gaillardia cleared his throat. "Firstly, I'd
like to thank everyone for making me so
welcome!" There were loud cheers—he was
a very popular fairy. "And secondly, I have
a very special message from an old friend,
delivered to me only this morning by a
friendly moorhen: *Greetings from far, far away!
I have reached my journey's end—a wonderful
flooded quarry, where humans like to swim and
dive with me. I wouldn't have made it without the
Flower Fairies' help. Thank you!*"

Willow knew at once that it was a message
from the pike. She smiled to herself.
Everything had turned out so well. The flood
was just a distant memory. The pike was safe
and well. And she had a brand-new friend.

She must be the happiest fairy in all Flower Fairyland.

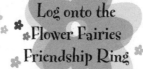

FLOWER
FAIRIES™
FRIENDS

Visit our Flower Fairies website at:

www.flowerfairies.com

There are lots of fun Flower Fairy games and
activities for you to play, plus you can find out more
about all your favorite fairy friends!

Log onto the
Flower Fairies
Friendship Ring

Visit the Flower Fairies website to sign up for the new
Flower Fairies Friendship Ring!

★ No membership fee
★ News and updates
★ Every new friend receives a special gift!
(while supplies last)